This Book Belongs to

OLIVVYH

For Bess, thanks for the inspiration.

D.C.

To Glenys and Christopher with love.

R.A.

Text copyright © 2010 by David Conway
Illustrations © 2010 by Roberta Angaramo
First published in Great Britain in 2009 by Gullane Children's Books
185 Fleet Street, London, EC4A 2HS
First published in the United States by HOLIDAY HOUSE, INC. in 2010
All Rights Reserved

"Sing a Rainbow" (from *Pete Kelly's Blues*)
Words and music by Arthur Hamilton
© 1955 (renewed) Mark VII Ltd
All rights administered by WB Music Corp.
All rights reserved. Used by permission of Alfred Publishing Co., Inc.

HOLIDAY HOUSE is registered in the U.S. Patent and Trademark Office.
Printed and Bound in November 2009 in Chachoengsao, Thailand, at Sirivatana Interprint Public Co., Ltd.
www.holidayhouse.com
First American Edition
1 3 5 7 9 10 8 6 4 2

Library of Congress Cataloging-in-Publication Data
Conway, David, 1970-
Errol and his extraordinary nose / by David Conway ; illustrated by Roberta Angaramo.—1st ed.
p. cm.
Summary: When his teacher announces a talent contest to raise money for his school,
Errol the elephant fears he has no unique skills to share.
ISBN 978-0-8234-2262-3 (hardcover)
[1. Elephants—Fiction. 2. Self-esteem—Fiction. 3. Talent shows—Fiction.
4. Schools—Fiction. 5. Animals—Fiction.]
I. Angaramo, Roberta, ill. II. Title.
PZ7.C76835Er 2010
[E]—dc22
2009025573

Errol
and His
Extraordinary Nose

by David Conway
illustrated by Roberta Angaramo

Holiday House / New York

All of the animals at Acacia Tree School had different
talents and they were always singing their own praises.
"I can swallow almost anything," bragged Abraham the Anaconda.
"If I was running with the herd you would
never spot me," boasted Zachary the Zebra.
"No matter what color it is, we can change
to match it," gloated the Chameleon Brothers . . .

. . . but none of the animals thought very much of Errol the Elephant. They thought he was awkward and clumsy and that his nose looked silly.

One day Mr. Geoffreys, the Giant Tortoise, made an announcement.
There was to be a talent contest to raise money for the school.

All of the animals were very excited.

All, that is, except Errol.
Everyone will just laugh at me, he thought.

Errol did his very best to
find a talent for the competition.

He tried **juggling**,
but his trunk got in the way. . . .

He tried **playing a musical instrument**,
but it sounded just AWFUL!

He even tried **dancing**,
but he was so heavy that he kept on falling over with a great big . . .

B U

By bedtime Errol was feeling very glum.
"I wish I was good at something," he said tearfully.
"There is nothing special about me."
"Now, now," said Errol's dad. "That's not true.
There is something special about everyone.

Everyone has a talent."

Then his dad gave him a book.
It was a book all about **elephants**.
"If you read this," he said, "you'll
soon see that there are lots of
things that are special about you."

Errol did indeed discover many interesting facts as he
settled down with the book that evening.
Facts like:

Elephants have excellent memories and
elephants can live to a very old age.

But most excitingly, Errol discovered that he was the owner of quite an
extraordinary nose.

It was a nose unlike any other in the animal kingdom,
a very versatile nose. A nose that could be used for . . .

reaching and grasping, . . .

spraying and drinking, and . . .

flinging and flailing, and . . .

snorkeling!

And a nose that could even be used like a periscope for sniffing out smells!

That night Errol felt very different as the dark
cloud that had been hanging over him drifted away.

The day of the talent contest finally
arrived, and Errol was feeling a little bit nervous.
But as he peered through a crack in the curtains,
he could see his dad in the audience, and
he remembered what he had told him.

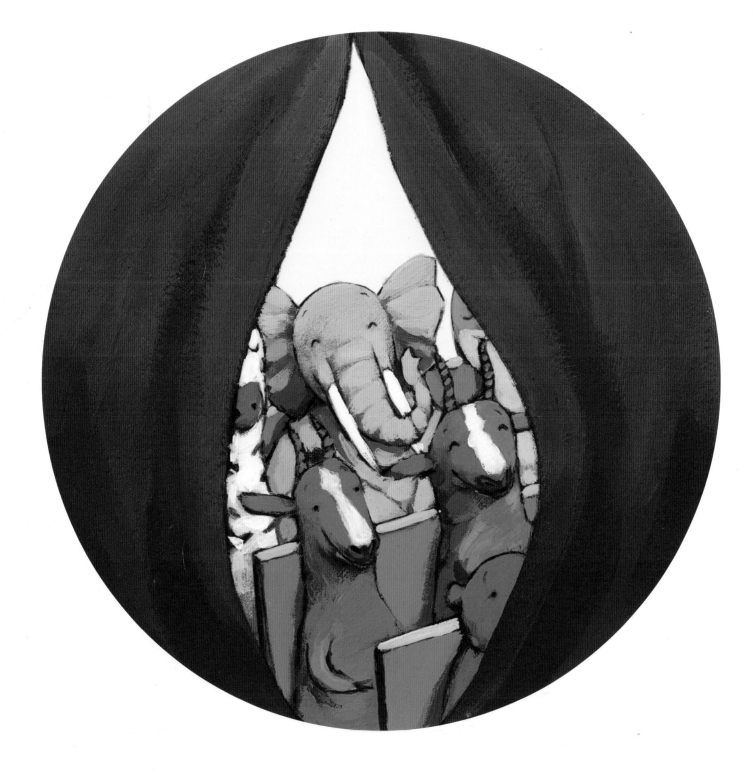

First up were the Chameleon Brothers, who sang a rendition of "Sing a Rainbow" while changing into lots of different colors.

Red and yellow and pink and green, purple and orange and blue.
We can sing a rainbow, sing a rainbow, sing a rainbow too. . . .

Then . . .

the African Finches sang in a choir . . .

while Morris the Meerkat conducted the orchestra!

Abraham the Anaconda ate two hundred pancakes . . .

and everyone tried their best to spot Zachary the Zebra.

At last it was Errol's turn to take to the stage.
He was still very nervous, but right away he . . .

amazed everyone as he reached and grasped objects just by using his nose.

And then he . . .

astounded everyone as he danced in a tank of water while using his nose as a snorkel.

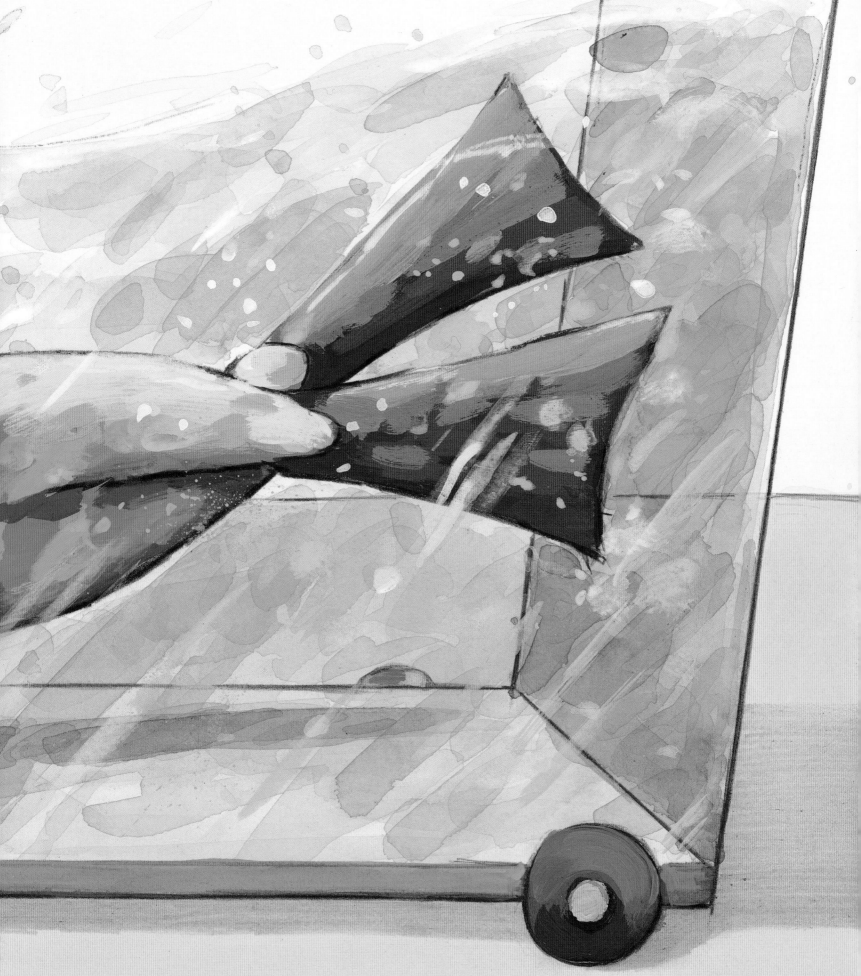

And then the whole audience was . . .

flabbergasted
when Errol created a beautiful
water and light show while singing a
song all about the rain!

When the talent contest had finished, everyone waited
in anticipation. Third place went to the Chameleon
Brothers for their colorful rendition of the rainbow song.
Second place went to Zachary the Zebra for being very hard to spot.

"And the winner," announced Mr. Geoffreys,
"and a well-deserved first place goes to . . .

Errol
and his Extraordinary Nose!"
The whole hall erupted as everyone cheered and clapped.

From that day on, none of the other animals at school thought little of Errol or his nose. In fact, Errol and his classmates discovered they shared the best talent of all . . .

making friends.